Chess!

I Love It I Love It I Love It!

OTHER TABLE TWO STORIES
BY JAMIE GILSON

Gotcha!

Bug in a Rug

It Goes Eeeeeeeeeeee!

Chess!

I Love It I Love It I Love It!

BY
JAMIE GILSON

ILLUSTRATED BY
AMY WUMMER

Clarion Books

New York

Clarion Books
a Houghton Mifflin Company imprint
215 Park Avenue South, New York, NY 10003
Text copyright © 2008 by Jamie Gilson
Illustrations copyright © 2008 by Amy Wummer

The illustrations were executed in ink and watercolor.
The text was set in 16-point Eureka Roman.

www.clarionbooks.com

Printed in the U.S.A.

Library of Congress Cataloging-in-Publication Data
Gilson, Jamie.
Chess! I love it I love it I love it! / by Jamie Gilson.
p. cm.
Summary: When second-grader Richard and three other members of the Sumac School
Chess Club compete in their first tournament, they each learn something about
luck, concentration, and teamwork.
ISBN 978-0-618-97790-1
[1. Chess—Fiction. 2. Competition (Psychology)—Fiction. 3. Schools—Fiction.]
I. Title.
PZ7.G4385Che 2008
[E]—dc22
2007040109

MP 10 9 8 7 6 5 4 3 2 1

For wonderful Noah,
who won trophies taller than he was

—J.G.

To Mark, who let me borrow his chess
set and answered all my questions

—A.W.

contents

one

Yucky

"**O**wwwww!" Patrick cried. He grabbed his arm and rolled under the playground slide. "You made me fall! You're gonna get it, Richard! *Owwwwwww!*" he went, louder. But he was faking. I could tell.

I jumped off the swing. "You saw me pumping," I told him. "You ran right in front of my feet. On purpose!"

"Did not!" he said.

"Did, too!" I said right back.

"You will definitely get it," he told me. "You cracked my elbow! See?" He stood up and showed me his arm. It was a little tiny bit red.

The first bell rang. All the kids on the playground headed inside. Patrick was hugging his arm like it would fall off. Now he was limping.

"I'm gonna tell," he said. Patrick likes getting kids in trouble, especially me. "I'll tell Mr. E and he'll get you. Big time."

Mr. E is vice principal at Sumac School. If you do something bad—like if you sneak a worm in somebody's lunch or, maybe, crack a kid's elbow—you get sent to Mr. E.

I've never been sent to Mr. E's office. Patrick has. Patrick is trouble. He's been in Mr. E's office three times. He always comes back smiling. He can talk his way out of trouble.

That's why I was scared. What if Mr. E really believed I'd messed up Patrick's elbow?

I followed Patrick. I hoped he wouldn't, but he headed for Mr. E's office. The door was open.

Two third graders raced past us. We had to jump out of their way.

"Freeze!" a voice behind us shouted. I froze. Patrick froze. All the kids in the hall froze. The voice was huge. It belonged to Mr. E.

"We. Do. Not. Run. In. The. Hall." the voice went, slow and quiet. "It is clearly dangerous."

Nobody made a sound. "Will the two boys who sped past my door come here. Now. Everyone else," he went on, "continue as you were."

We unfroze and watched the two kids shuffle back toward Mr. E's office. I was glad I wasn't them.

Patrick hugged his arm again. "You just wait," he whispered.

We walked very slowly down the hall. Patrick had stopped limping. I waved to some kids in the other second-grade classroom. Then I threw my jacket in my locker. Just as the last bell rang, we headed into Mrs. Zookey's room. She's our teacher.

Patrick sat right down at Table Three. I sit at Table Two. When I walked past, he stuck out his foot and tried to trip me. He tries that a lot, but he never gets me. I always hop over it.

All through the Pledge and lunch count he held his arm. Then it was time for Yummys and Yuckys. We do them every Monday. If Mrs. Zookey calls on you and you tell a good thing, that's a Yummy. A bad thing is a Yucky.

Patrick leaned his chair back toward me. "Watch this," he said.

He raised his good arm high. "Me! Me! Me first!" he called. "I've got a Yucky." He looked straight at me. "I've got a terrible, stinky, awful Yucky!"

"No, Mrs. Zookey, me!" said Dawn Marie. She raised her arm higher than Patrick's.

But Mrs. Zookey went first. "Here's a sweet-smelling Yummy." She held up a bunch of big red roses. "All this month, we'll be learning about flowers. I expect you can smell these from here." She smiled, like that was the all-time best Yummy.

When Mrs. Zookey looked away, Patrick held his nose. "Flowers are for girls," he whispered.

Some kids leaned toward the roses. I sniffed. Smelled good to me.

My friend Ben sits next to me at Table Two. He had his hand up, and I knew why. His dad got him a very cool bike horn that looks like Godzilla, and he wanted to tell about it. It raises its paws and roars. *GROAAARRR!*

Mrs. Zookey looked at all the hands. I hoped she would pick Ben or Dawn Marie.

"Me!" Patrick called again. "Please, please, me!" He waved both arms. He looked like a duck taking off from a lake.

"Oh, Patrick," said Mrs. Zookey. "So much energy. Indeed, you were the first to ask. Next time, though, you will sit still and listen. Do you hear?"

Patrick smiled. He didn't care about next time. *This* time, he had won.

That's what he thought. He was flapping his arms like crazy. *Both* of them.

"Patrick," I whispered, "how's your elbow? Is it cracked?"

He grabbed his arm quick, but it was too late.

"Go ahead, Patrick," Mrs. Zookey said. "Tell us your terrible, stinky, awful Yucky."

He bit his lip. "On the playground," he started.

I waved both my arms, just like he had.

"On the playground," he started again, "Richard made me fall down and—"

"By accident," I said.

"Oh," said Mrs. Zookey. "I'm sorry you had a spill, Patrick. Do you need to see the nurse?"

Patrick shrugged and crossed his arms. When she looked away, he stuck out his tongue at me.

"I win!" I told myself.

"Ophelia." Mrs. Zookey pointed to her. "Why don't you go next."

Ophelia shook her long red hair and bit her lip like this was going to be bad stuff. She stood up.

"Wait, wait, sit down," Patrick said. "Wait. *That*'s not my Yucky. I was just getting started." You could tell he was trying to think of something else terrible, stinky, and awful.

"See," he went on, "my father and me, we play chess. And here's my real Yucky. He never lets me win. And that's no fair. I can beat anybody else, though," he said, "if I want to."

"Can *not*," Ben whispered to me.

"Can *not!*" I said out loud.

"Richard." Mrs. Zookey turned to me. "You play chess. Do you win every time?"

"I beat my mom once last week," I told her. "But that was because the macaroni was burning. She's good. But lots of kids beat Patrick. I mean it."

Patrick stared at me and then made like he was sticking his finger down his throat.

"ACHOOOO!" Ophelia sneezed. It was a shower. She could have put out a fire with it. Mrs. Zookey gave her a tissue.

"Wait. It morphs into a Yummy," Patrick told the class. "My father showed me some secret stuff. I'm going to play Mr. E at Chess Club today. And I'm gonna smash him."

Ben, Ophelia, and I laughed out loud. If there was any secret stuff in chess, Mr. E already knew it.

"His name is Mr. Economopoulos," Mrs. Zookey said. "Everyone, say his name once again, so you'll remember: E-con-o-mop-ou-los."

She always makes us say it, but everybody else just calls him Mr. E. He says that's okay.

It fits him, too. Mr. E is a "Myster-E." He does tricks. He can make a chess piece disappear in his hand. Then suddenly it appears behind your ear. He can also make your mom show up at school. And nobody, *nobody* smashes him at chess.

Late last September, Mr. E started Chess Club. It meets on Mondays after school. Ben and I had played each other since we were six, so we signed up. Thirteen kids did. Four of us are from Mrs. Zookey's class—Ben, me, Ophelia, and Patrick.

A lot of kids still didn't get it. Tess, a kid at Table Four, raised her hand. "Isn't chess hard? I always thought going to Chess Club was like going to school after school."

"Yeah," Sam said. He sits next to her. "My brother says you've got to be really smart and that I should forget about it."

"No way," I told them. "It's a *game*. It's fun. You should try it."

Any other after-school club, you start in and do stuff, like fold origami or build towers with toothpicks. But first thing when he gets to Chess Club, Mr. E raises his arms over his head and he yells, "Chess!"

Then we all have to pump our fists and yell, "I love it I love it I love it!"

Chess really is fun. I guess I love it, but I could be better at it. I wish I was.

"Well, if I don't crush Mr. E," Patrick said, "at least I'll get Richard. For sure."

"No way," I told him. But, okay, he might. If his dad did play great chess, maybe he had taught Patrick secret stuff. In the library there are stacks of books on how to play. And there are, like, a gazillion different moves you can make.

Patrick was grinning again like he was King of the Mountain.

"Thank you, Patrick, and good luck," Mrs.

Zookey told him. "Now, Ophelia, what do you have for us?"

Ophelia stood up again. She was not smiling. I hoped it wasn't going to be another dead gerbil. She already had two. The last one was called Binky. She had told us how she buried Binky in a cracker box. That was a big-time Yucky. The next week her grandma got her a new gerbil. That was a Yummy.

She shifted from one foot to the other. "This is very not good," she said. She sneezed and rubbed her nose with the soggy tissue.

I held my ears. Some Yuckys are *too* yucky.

"You know what?" she asked us. I could hear even with my ears covered.

Nobody knew what.

"I've got to be a flower girl, that's what. At my second cousin Mary Jo's wedding a week from Saturday."

I unheld my ears. It wasn't all *that* yucky.

Holly raised her hand. "I was a flower girl once," she said. "I got to dress up like a princess."

"Why, Ophelia, you'll be wonderful," Mrs. Zookey said. She sounded happy. I bet she had thought it was going to be a dead gerbil, too.

"No," Ophelia said. "I will not be wonderful. I don't like Mary Jo. She talks baby talk at me. And you know what else? She's getting married at Heeby-Jeeby Amusement Park. And I *won't* get to dress up. Everybody—even the flower girl—has to wear a red checked shirt and blue jeans. And—"

Patrick broke in. "That's nothing. I heard about people who got married jumping out of an airplane. They wore parachutes."

"Patrick!" Mrs. Zookey warned.

Ophelia put her hands on top of her head, like she was trying to hold it on. "The thing is, Heeby-Jeeby is where they got engaged. It was on the Whirly-Wheel. You know."

We all knew. The Whirly-Wheel was scary. It was high. It was fast. It was famous.

"Well," Ophelia went on, "after they get married in the picnic tent, they're going to ride on it. And I'm supposed to throw this great big bag of pink rose petals from the very top of the Whirly-Wheel." She sneezed again and wiped her nose on her sleeve.

"I've been on that thing a hundred million times," Patrick said. "No biggie. I never even hold on."

"I love the Whirly-Wheel," a kid at Table Three said. "It's awesome."

"I know. I know it's easy for everybody else," Ophelia said. "I only rode it once. You know what happened?" she asked us.

Nobody knew, but we could guess.

She took a deep breath. "I threw up," she told us. "All over the place."

"Eee-yew," everybody went.

"My mom says if I don't eat eggs that morning, I'll be okay," Ophelia said. "But I won't be okay. My little sister Bea loves the Whirly-Wheel. She says I'm a scaredy-cat. And she's only five and three-quarter years old. So that's my Yucky." She sat down and crossed her arms.

"What a wimp," Patrick whispered.

"Throwing up is no fun," said Mrs. Zookey. She patted Ophelia's shoulder. "Why don't you ask them if you can scatter the petals on the merry-go-round instead? Heeby-Jeeby has a nifty one, with endangered animals that go up and down quite slowly. I'm sure that wouldn't upset your stomach. I can just picture it—the bride and groom riding on the giant Chinese paddlefish, pink rose petals flying all around."

Ophelia sneezed.

Quickly, Mrs. Zookey grabbed a stack of papers and started handing them out. "Write your name at the top," she said, "and then answer this question: Why do plants have flowers? At the end of the flower unit you'll do it again, and you'll see how very much you've learned.

"And next Monday," she went on, "let's try to have more Yummys and fewer Yuckys, okay?"

She started drawing a flower on the chalkboard.

"I'm not sure if mine's a Yummy or a Yucky," Dawn Marie whispered to Ben and me. "Yesterday we got a dog from the animal shelter. He's a cockerdoodle. That's part cocker spaniel and part poodle."

"Wow! What could be yucky about that?" Ben asked her. "My mom's a cat person. She says I can't have a dog, not even one that looks a little like a cat."

"I never heard of a cockerdoodle," I said. "Maybe I could see him sometime. Dogs like me."

"He likes *me* so much," she said, "he thinks my toes are doggy treats. He nips. And when he's not

nipping, he barks and runs around in circles."
Dawn Marie shook her head. "He never stops. All
last night he whined and he barked. He barked
and he whined. He drove me batty."

"Here's what you do," Ben told her. "You look
him in the eye and you say, 'Sit! Stay! Good dog!'
And you use his name," Ben said. "You didn't tell
us. What is it?"

"I don't know," Dawn Marie said. "He hasn't
got one yet."

"I know," I told her. "You could call him
Patrick."

two

Hip, Hip, Hooray for Harry!

At a quarter to three, the "School's Out" bell rang. Ben and I grabbed our backpacks and headed straight to the Art Room. That's where Chess Club meets.

A bunch of third and fourth graders were already there setting up their pieces. The Chess Club keeps its stuff on a shelf in the Art Room, so we don't have to bring anything.

Ben pulled out one of the rubbery roll-up chessboards. I grabbed a green bag of chess pieces. The tables were sticky with paste, so we set up on the floor. Ben picked a black bishop and a white bishop out of the pile and put them behind his back. "Which hand?" he asked me.

"Left."

It was the black bishop. That meant I was playing with the black pieces. I sorted them out.

On each end of the first row I put the rooks. They look like castles. Next to them went my knights. I like knights best because they are the only pieces that can jump over other pieces. They jump in this L-shape.

After them go the bishops. Then, in the middle of the row, the queen and the king. The king is a big deal. If he gets trapped, you lose. That's it. Game over.

In the row in front of them I counted out my eight pawns.

Ready to go.

"Good luck," I told Ben, and we shook hands. It's what you do every time you play.

"Good luck," he said, and he grinned. "You'll need it."

"When cockerdoodles fly," I told him, and laughed.

He moved first because white always does. It's the rule.

Patrick got there just as Shasha skipped in. She's the only kindergartener in the club. "I haven't played you in a month, Shasha," Patrick told her. "Today I'm going to smash you." She just laughed.

Shasha must be the littlest kid in kindergarten. She looks kind of like a doll because she wears these dresses with ruffles and ribbons. Patrick could smash her easy if he sat on her. But not at chess. She keeps getting better.

Last time I played her, she beat me. I bet Patrick didn't know how good she'd gotten. I bet he thought she'd be out in four moves.

Suddenly, the Art Room door opened wide and Mr. E filled it. He's as tall as a basketball player. I bet his Sumac School sweatshirt is XXXXXXXL.

"Chess!" he shouted, and he raised his arms up high. He looked like a giant Y.

We all jumped to our feet. We pumped our fists over our heads and called out, "I love it I love it I love it!"

"Cool," said Mr. E. "So do I." He threw one arm up again, and this time a bunch of black and white paper flowers appeared in his hand.

"How do you *do* that?" a third-grade kid asked

him. Mr. E just smiled. It's the kind of stuff he does in Chess Club.

"But wait!" he called out. He tossed the flowers onto one of the art desks. "Don't sit down. Time to loosen up those lazy fingers. Can you send brain waves down to them? Let's see."

See what? We looked at each other. Lazy fingers? Brain waves? Usually we play till he gets there. Then he starts out with a lesson. He hangs up this big chessboard with pockets for the pieces and shows us different moves.

But this wasn't going to be a lesson day. Instead, Mr. E did this rap. I think it was rap. It was fast. He did it with hand motions.

First, he slapped his hands on his chest and said, "Chess Club, did you 'ear" (he pointed to both his ears) "about Harry?" (He rubbed his fingers on his bearded chin.)

I got it. "Chest" sounds like "chess." "Ear" sounds like "hear." His chin is hairy. He was saying, "Chess Club, did you hear about Harry?" Ben and I laughed a little just to be nice, and started to sit down. But Mr. E went on.

"He just" (he rubbed his chest again) "got back" (quick, he moved his hands behind him) "from the tourn-a-ment" (and he turned like a top). "I 'ear" (he pointed again) "he knows" (he pushed his nose way flat) "how to squish" (he stamped his foot) "his foes. Hip, hip!" (he pounded them) "hooray!" (arms in the air) "for Harry!" He rubbed his chin again. And again.

We laughed. We laughed until he said to us, "Fine. Now you do it. You can rub the tops of your heads for Harry." There isn't any hair on the top of Mr. E's head. He shaves it all off.

"No way," one of the fourth graders told him. "I want to play chess."

"And so you shall," said Mr. E. "After two times through as fast as you can."

"Chess Club," we began. Then we tried to follow him all the way through the pats and rubs. "Did you 'ear about *Har*-ry. *Just* got *back* from the *tourn*-a-ment. *I 'ear* he *knows* how to *squish* his foes. *Hip, hip,* hooray! for *Har*-ry!"

We tried, but we couldn't keep up. He moved too fast. My brain couldn't talk to my fingers at all.

After two times, Ben and I fell down on the floor, laughing. A lot of kids just quit.

"Concentration," said Mr. E. "What this takes,

like chess, is concentration. And practice. Lots of practice."

"Mr. E! Mr. E!" Patrick called. "Tournament! You said tournament. My mother says it's time I played in a tournament."

"And right she is, young Mr. P.," Mr. E told him. "In fact, I have an important announcement. Wait'll you hear this. I was visiting Maple School today. That's where I heard about Harry. The chess club there is going to have a tournament . . . and we're going to enter. How about that?"

"We'll rule!" Patrick shouted.

Ben went, "Wow!"

Ophelia threw her arms in the air. "I love it I love it I love it!" she said. Most kids *ya-hoo*ed.

I wasn't all that sure. I let a kindergartner beat me last week. How was I going to do against really, really good players?

"There are a lot of serious tournaments," Mr. E told us. "But this isn't one of them. It's just for fun, but there'll be trophies. The clubs from all five schools in town are invited," he went on. "Most of the kids, like you, won't ever have been in a tournament. So. How many of you've got the stuff to represent Sumac a week from Saturday morning? We can enter as many as ten players."

A week from Saturday . . . what was happening a week from this Saturday? I couldn't think of anything except me and Ben scaring little kids and squirrels with his Godzilla horn.

Ben looked at me. "Why not?" he asked. He raised his hand. Most kids did. I put mine up halfway.

"Good. Good." Mr. E nodded. "You check at home and report back to my office tomorrow morning. I have a lot of school things going on, so leave me a note if I'm busy.

"Today, since it's almost tournament time, I'll just watch you play. But I want you to remember all the lessons you've learned—especially last week's on opening moves. Vary those openings. Some of you want to start every game with the same piece. And don't bring your queen out too early."

We'd been doing this for maybe six months and we'd learned a lot about opening moves, checkmates, and everything in between. Ben and I were getting better. Some kids, like Ophelia, were getting really good.

When Mr. E bent over the guys next to us, he

said, "Okay, you know the drill. What do you do when you see a good move?"

The kid had his fingers out, ready to jump a knight. He pulled his arm back. "Sit on my hand until I see a better one," he said.

Mr. E tells us that all the time.

"Exactly," he said.

I stared at our board. "You think he's got me?" I asked Mr. E.

"What's the first thing you do to find out?"

"Check out the whole board," I said.

Mr. E tells us that all the time.

"Castle if you can, and I think you can," he said.

I could, and I did! Castling is neat. You get to move your rook and king on the same turn. The king ends up closer to the corner. He's safer there.

"Mr. E, I forgot," a third grader told him. "We've got a huge soccer game that Saturday. Huge. If I skip it, my coach will kill me." All the fourth graders said so, too.

"Kill you? Wow!" Mr. E slapped his head. "Then you couldn't play soccer *or* chess. Okay, so how many does that leave us?"

Ben and I put up our hands. So did Shasha.

"I'll be there," Patrick said. He flew one of his bishops high, like it was a jet. "Ha!" he went. Then he swooped it down and knocked over one of Shasha's pawns. "My mother already has a shelf for all the trophies I'm going to win."

"I'll be there, too," Ophelia said. "I'll—" Then she moaned. "Oh, no! That's the Saturday I'll be throwing up at the wedding."

This was not so good. Ophelia is a cool player. She's beaten everybody in the club, even the fourth graders.

"Mr. E! Mr. E!" Patrick called. "I've just about creamed Shasha. Now can I play you? I've got this trick. My father used it on me last night. He creamed me."

I wondered how come Patrick was beating Shasha so fast. I leaned over to look.

Mr. E looked, too. Then he smiled at Shasha.

She smiled back. Slowly, she slid her bishop across the squares. She picked up Patrick's queen and tossed it to him. "Checkmate," she said.

Patrick blinked. He shook his head. Shasha had trapped his king. She had won. She had beat him. That was that.

Patrick started to laugh, like he was really the

winner. "She's barely five years old," he said. "I wasn't even trying."

"Six," Shasha told him. "I just turned six."

"Check," Ben called out. That didn't mean our game was over. It did mean his rook would get my king if I didn't stop him. It was hard to think and listen to Patrick at the same time.

I slid my king down behind a pawn, where it was safer. I could tell, though, that this was going to be a short game.

"Patrick," Mr. E said, "you can try your tricks on Ben when he's finished his match. See if they work. But remember, chess isn't a game of tricks. It's a game of careful planning."

Shasha stuck out her hand. Patrick took it like it was a wet sock. "Good game," she said.

"Good game," he mumbled. And it had been—for her.

"There's something you need to know," Mr. E said. "I have a warning for all of you in the tournament. It's about Harry. I 'ear he knows how to squish his foes." He put his hands around his throat. "Beware, beware of Harry!"

"No kidding?" I asked Mr. E. "There's a real Harry?"

"You'd better believe it," he said. "I bet Harry is why Maple School is having this tournament. But I think we'll surprise them. Get to work and show me your stuff."

"Checkmate," Ben said. He zapped me. "You could have blocked me with your knight, see?" He pointed. "You could have gotten me." He was right, too. I just hadn't seen it.

The room got quiet. Kids won, kids lost, and kids moved on to play other kids. When he was playing Ben, Patrick stood up and yelled, "No, no, *no! That's* not what you were supposed to do!"

Ben just smiled.

"Ah, Patrick, thinking players don't often fall for tricks," Mr. E told him.

Ben slid his bishop across the board. "Check," he said. Two moves later, it was over.

"No fair," said Patrick.

Then Ophelia beat Patrick really fast. I had an idea about what was happening. Patrick was mad about losing to Shasha and Ben. When he's mad, he goes ballistic, and all he can think about is being mad.

I lost, too, to this third grader. Mr. E watched me go down the drain.

"Mr. E," I told him, "losing's no fun. I don't want to keep losing."

"Losing hurts," Mr. E said, "but you *know* what you need to do. I've seen you play cool, smart games, Richard. You can do it."

By then it was 4:15. "Time's up, group," Mr. E announced. "Next Monday we'll get ready for the tournament. Until then, I want you all to do your chess puzzles and practice, practice, practice."

He pulled a batch of puzzles off the chess shelf and passed them out. They show pictures of a board with a game going on. You have to decide what to do next. Under the pictures it says stuff like, "Can Black checkmate? If so, how would you do it?"

I like puzzles, but I like playing with my own chess set most of all.

"Mr. E!" I raised my hand. "Next week, can I bring my lucky chess set?"

"Me, too," Patrick said. "I've got a brand-new one that's luckier than Richard's."

"There's no luck to winning," Mr. E told us. "You know that. Still, if you think it will help, bring all the sets you want."

The next thing he did was magic. He picked up the black and white flowers and reached for the ceiling. "Hip, hip, hooray for Team Sumac!" he yelled, and the flowers turned into bumblebees.

three

Bad Dog
and
Godzilla

That whole week Ben and I were chess maniacs. Every day we did chess puzzles. Every day we played killer games. I won maybe half of them. Most of the time we used my lucky chess set.

It's a great set. My mom gave it to me when I was in kindergarten. She taught me how to play on it.

When I was really little, like two or three, Mom and I used to sing, "Old MacDonald had a farm. *E-I-E-I-O.*"

I liked to go, "And on this farm there lived a Skunk. *E-I-E-I-O.* With a Pee-yew here and a Pee-yew there. Here a Pee. There a Yew. Everywhere a Pee-yew."

Okay, sometimes we still sing it.

Anyway, my mom found an Old MacDonald set on a chess website. It has Old MacDonald. He's the king. Mrs. Old MacDonald is the queen. Two cows with spots are the bishops. The knights are pigs. They are smiling. Red barns are the rooks.

The pawns were chickens. Mom threw them away. Then she went to this pottery place. She made sixteen brand-new pawns out of clay. She painted them and baked them. They're not just any old pawns, either. They're skunks. No joke. Skunks. The eight black skunks have white stripes. The eight white skunks have black stripes. I bet nobody ever saw a skunk pawn before.

Ben roared his bike up to my house Sunday afternoon, honking his Godzilla horn. Every squirrel on the block hid. But we didn't go out riding. No, sir. Ben just propped his bike against a tree in my front yard and came inside.

What we did was sit right down at the kitchen table. I set up the board and we played. Ben likes plain old chess pieces best, but at my house he plays with Old Mac.

"I don't know who Harry is," I said after a while, "but I bet we smear him, just like I'm about to smear you." One of my cows was staring down one of his skunks.

Just then the front doorbell rang.

"Uh-oh. If it's Patrick, what do we do?" I asked Ben. Patrick lives across the street. He rings our bell all the time. Then sometimes he runs. Ding Dong Ditch.

"If he rings again, we hide," Ben said, and that sounded good to me.

The bell rang again.

Mom was in the kitchen, too. She was making banana bread. "Answer the door," she said. "If it's Patrick, you'll invite him in and you'll behave."

With Patrick, that's hard to do. Patrick is always trouble.

Ben and I both went to the front door. I figured it wouldn't hurt to check, so I opened up the mail slot. I peeked out. SLURP. A fat, wet tongue licked my face.

It was not Patrick's tongue.

The tongue belonged to Dawn Marie's no-name cockerdoodle.

I wiped the dog spit off my face and opened the door. Ben and I went out to look.

The dog was big and brown with white spots. He yipped. He barked. He jumped on us. He ran around in circles. His ears flapped. Dawn Marie was tugging at his leash.

"He's still a little hyper," she said. "I'm trying to teach him to sit. Sit!"

The dog did not sit. He kept yipping. He kept barking. He kept running around in circles.

"That," a kid yelled out, "is the loudest dog I ever heard!"

The kid was Patrick. He came across the street and stopped at our maple tree.

"I was just about to beat my dad at chess," he told us, "but it got so loud out here, I had to see what was going on." He stepped back. "I think that dog's part werewolf."

"Patrick!" his father called from across the street. "You give up?"

Patrick sighed. "Guess who was winning?" he asked us.

"Patrick?" his father called again.

"I want to play with this crazy dog!" Patrick yelled back. "Let's call it a draw."

"A draw? You call that a draw? You better come back and practice for your tournament," Patrick's father said, and went inside.

The dog sat down in front of Ben.

"Good dog," said Ben, and he leaned down to pet him.

"*Yip,*" went the dog. "*Arf,*" went the dog. He stood up. He wagged his tail. Then he began to run around Ben.

"Sit!" said Ben. "Stay!"

Ben kept turning, trying to look the dog in the eye. But the dog kept running around him. The leash was totally tying up his ankles.

"He's too fast for me," Dawn Marie said. She dropped her end of the leash and threw up her hands.

"Stay, dog!" Ben was yelling now. He tried to grab the leash, but he was losing his balance.

"*ARF! ARF!*" the dog barked, like he thought this was a great game.

"That dog's way too loud," Patrick said. "But I bet *this* is louder than he is." He reached out to Ben's bike, which was still propped against the tree.

"No!" Ben yelled. "Don't do that!"

But he did. Patrick squeezed the trigger of the horn on Ben's bike. Twice. Ben's Godzilla raised up its paws and went "GROAAARR! GROAAARR!"

The dog stopped barking. He stopped yipping. But he did not stop running. He bolted away from Patrick and the monster horn, yanking Ben by his ankles.

"Bad dog! Bad dog!" Dawn Marie yelled.

I threw myself at the hyper dog, trying to grab him as he went by. But I just ended up skidding on the grass.

When the dog and Ben got to the sidewalk, the dog pulled hard one way. Ben pulled hard the other. It looked for a minute like Ben had him, but then Ben stumbled.

KAPOW! He crashed to the concrete. The dog had won the tug of war.

Ben fell down like a bowling pin. He fell face first.

I was sure he'd get a bloody nose, but he didn't. It was worse. He lifted his head and you could see. It was one of his front teeth. Part of it was missing. Chipped off. The part that was left was sharp. Like Dracula's.

As soon as Patrick saw it he went, "Aargh," and he ran. "Gotta get home!" he yelled.

A tiny triangle of tooth sparkled on the sidewalk.

It must have hurt a lot because Ben's eyes were all filled up with water. "That was bad, you bad, *bad* dog," he said.

The no-name cockerdoodle came over and licked his face.

"Sit," said Dawn Marie. The dog sat and wagged his tail. He must have thought the game was over.

"Ben," I asked, "are you okay?"

"Sort of," he said. He sat up, touched the sharp tip of his tooth, and shook his head. Then he began to unwind the leash from his ankles.

"What happened?" Patrick called from the steps of his house. At least he didn't say "Gotcha!"

"Oh, come on," I told him. "You did that on purpose."

"It wasn't me," Patrick called back. "It was Godzilla. He's a mean one."

Patrick is too much. If I beat him up, my mom would ground me for a year. If I beat him in chess, though, that would be okay. And he'd be really sorry.

four

Harry
Is Who?

Monday morning, Ben got the first Yucky. He kept his mouth shut. Then he stuck out his tongue with his mouth open. It was just a little chip, but you could see it. "I am zee Count Dracula," he said in a spooky voice.

Everyone went, "Eee-yew!"

"It wasn't *my* fault," said Patrick. But nobody said it was. Ben didn't even tell on the dog.

The rest of the Y-and-Y's were pretty lame. They were all Yummys. A Table Four kid had learned to whistle the first line of "Jingle Bells," which is not all that hard because it's mostly just one note. Dawn Marie had named her dog. "He's called Zilly," she told us. "That's short for Godzilla."

Patrick raised his hand. Mrs. Zookey called on him. "Zilly?" he asked. "You know what that is? Silly." We all groaned.

I had brought my chess set to school, but I hid it in my locker. I wanted to surprise the kids at Chess Club.

"We learned a lot about flowers last week," Mrs. Zookey said, "but today we're going to study a different kind." She held up a big yellow dandelion.

"That's not a flower, it's a weed," someone told her.

"Ah-ha," said Mrs. Zookey. "Can't it be both? What's a weed?"

"It's something you don't want in your yard," I said. "It's a pest." I was staring straight at Patrick.

Then we had to look in our reference books and write down Five Fun Facts about dandelions. I broke the point of my pencil. When I went to sharpen it, Patrick stuck out his foot, and this time he almost got me.

After school, I was the first one in the Art

Room for Chess Club. Ben couldn't come. He was at the dentist.

First, I brushed a bunch of silver sparkle off a table. Then I set up my board on it. I put all the Old MacDonald pieces in their places. Everybody was going to love it.

When she saw it, Shasha, the kindergarten whiz, said, "I love it." She picked the white cow from my right fist, shook my hand, went "Good luck," sat down, and slid one of the white skunk pawns two spaces forward.

It was great. The kids who came in watched us play. "Hog heaven!" a fourth grader yelled when Shasha picked up her pig knight.

"Shasha knows how to squish her foes," a kid sang. "Hip, hip, hooray for Shasha!" But I was about to be the squisher. I was sure of it.

Mr. E opened the door and came in. This time he waved a black wand. In a big booming voice, he called out, "Chess!"

We all stood up, pumped our fists, and yelled, "I love it I love it I love it!" That's when something small and white flew out of the wand. Mr. E caught it in his left hand and showed it to us. It was a knight.

"Wow!" we all went.

"Magic," Mr. E told us, "is something that seems impossible but isn't. This magic knight," he said, "wants to help someone win at chess who isn't so sure he can."

We all laughed. But suddenly, he reached behind my ear, lifted out the knight, and dropped it in my hand.

"Looks like this time he's chosen Richard," Mr. E said.

Some of the kids came to look. The knight was

maybe two inches tall. The horse he was sitting on had a missing leg. He didn't look magic. He looked broken.

When the kids went back to their games, Mr. E told me, "Richard, the knight can help you win. Keep him close and listen to what he tells you."

"Thank you," I said. "I guess." I closed my left fist around the white knight. I didn't hear anything.

As the kids played their first games, Mr. E unrolled his big teaching board and hung it on some wall hooks. You could see the pieces he'd set up in their clear plastic pockets.

"Okay, players," he said finally, "let me have your attention. I want you to take a look at the white bishop." He pointed to it. "What's going on here?"

Ophelia raised her hand. "It's a *fork*," she said. "That bishop is attacking the king and a rook at the same time." She was right, too.

We talked a lot about forks and skewers and other cool chess stuff, and then we started to play again.

Shasha was making her move. Mrs. Old

MacDonald was about to attack one of my cows, so I slid a skunk up to protect it.

"I see you took the magic knight's advice," Mr. E told me. "You used your pawn for defense. That's the way."

It wasn't the magic knight, though. It was me.

"Terrific farm set," he went on. "I've got one at home with baseball players. The pitcher is the king, and the umpire is the queen."

The room was quiet for at least ten minutes. Mr. E circled around watching games and asking kids questions about their moves.

And that's when Patrick rushed in.

"You're late," Mr. E told him. "Late is not good."

"But look," said Patrick, holding out a shoebox. "Just see what I've got. I was only late because I was waiting for it. My mother brought it over." Most of the kids stopped playing to look.

"Check," I told Shasha. I had made this really cool move while she was staring at Patrick.

She slid her red barn over to keep her Old MacDonald safe. But it wasn't enough. Two moves later Old MacDonald was trapped.

"Checkmate," I called. I won.

She stared at the board. "How'd I let you do that?" she asked. She shook my hand. "Good game," she said. "Really. Your cows and skunks kicked my sheep and pigs."

I smiled. She was pretty good, but she made mistakes, too.

"Who wants to play me?" Patrick called out. "Just wait'll you see this. Is that your kindergarten set, Shasha?" he asked when he spotted it.

She shook her head.

"It's mine," I told him, and he started to laugh.

"What's so funny?" I asked him.

"Piggies and moo-cows. Ha!"

He opened his shoebox. Then he took the pieces out one by one and put them on an empty table. Every kid in the club came to look, but he wouldn't let them touch his set. It was amazing.

"Zowie!" Mr. E said. "Those look ferocious."

Patrick laughed some more.

It wasn't funny. My pieces looked nice and friendly. His pieces looked mean. They had their jaws wide open so you could see their pointy little teeth. You could almost hear them roar like Godzilla. They were dinosaurs!

"Everybody back to their games," Mr. E said. "I think we've got a good matchup here. Richard, you're free. And you and Patrick both have the same problems. We've talked about them before. Both of you need to concentrate. Both of you need to plan ahead. Let's see you do it."

This was not true. Patrick was a goof-off and I was getting better. We weren't the same. But you don't talk back to Mr. E.

When Mr. E moved on to the next board, Patrick went, "He's all wrong. *All* wrong. No way I'm like you. I get bad luck. *You* just can't play."

"That's what *you* think," I said. I held tight to the magic knight. Maybe he *had* helped me beat Shasha. "I'll show you. Come on, let's play with my set."

"No way," he told me. "It's for babies. You've got to play with mine."

"No way right back," I said. "This is my lucky set."

Mr. E heard us. "Why don't you each use your own pieces?" he asked.

"I like it!" Patrick said. "My triceratops will eat his piggy for breakfast."

"Okay by me. My skunks will take on your dino-egg pawns anytime," I told him. "But we've got to use my board. And I get to be white so I can start. That's it."

"O*kay*." Patrick smiled. "Why not?" He leaned over so his nose just about touched my nose. "GROAAARRR!" he roared.

"GROAAARRR!" I roared right back. I wanted to beat him so bad. "I'm gonna . . ." I opened my hand, and the white knight dropped on the floor. "GROAAARRR!" I went again.

"Enough roaring. Enough!" Mr. E said. "Get your heads in the game. Theo, are you without a partner?" he asked a fourth grader. "Set up your board, and I'll play you. Onward, group! You can be sure that Harry is practicing right now."

In between moves, Mr. E went from board to board, giving everybody advice.

"Don't take that rook just because you can," he told a kid. "What happens to your queen if you take it?" The kid sat on his hands. "Always, *always* remember to make the best move, not the easiest."

He was always, *always* saying that.

Mr. E stopped to play Theo's board, and then he moved on.

I slid one of my middle skunks toward Patrick. "Dinosaurs were dumb, you know," I told him. "They had teeny brains."

"Maybe," he said. "But just one of their toes could mash your skunk like a worm on the sidewalk. Ha!"

I didn't want Mr. E to see the magic white knight on the floor, so I bent down to get it. It wasn't there. When I sat back up, Patrick said, "You touched your pig. I saw it. Mr. E, he touched his pig! That's the rule. You touch it, you move it."

"Did not," I said.

"Did, too," he went.

Mr. E had warned us. At tournaments, when you touch a piece, you have to move it unless you call out "Adjust." When I bent over, I held on to the edge of the table. Maybe I'd touched the pig a little. It was too late for me to yell out "Adjust."

I nudged the pig onto another square. One of his dinosaurs gobbled it up.

Patrick was making me mad. I knew this wasn't good. I had to think.

I could shake up Patrick if I took a long time moving. It had worked before. So I looked at the ceiling and whistled "E-I-E-I-O." I tried to plan three moves ahead, but I couldn't even think of one.

While I was doing that, Patrick told kids how much his mom paid for the set. He also told them how stinky skunks are.

The kids said, "Shhh."

"Zip it up, Patrick," said Mr. E.

After that, Patrick just whispered. He sure wasn't thinking about the game. This was good. But I couldn't stop listening to him. Not so good.

He captured one of my cows and put it on top of his head. "My T-rex just took your moo-cow. Ha!"

It didn't take him very long. He beat me.

"Good game," I said. I shook his hand.

"I rule!" he said. He squeezed my knuckles.

Then I played a fourth grader, and Ophelia went dinosaur-to-dinosaur with Patrick. She squashed him.

"I've won every single match today," she told

Mr. E. "I wish I could play Saturday. My mom keeps saying I'll be fine at the dumb wedding."

"Well, you're certainly in fine form today," Mr. E told her.

"Maybe," she said, "but, you know, Patrick's always easy."

Patrick stuck out his tongue at her.

Patrick's chess set didn't turn out to be so lucky.

Neither did mine. And the magic knight was missing.

At four o'clock, Mr. E said, "Okay, Team Sumac, stick around. I have a surprise for you. The rest of you can be on your way."

After the other kids left, he took his cell phone out, punched in a number, and said something we couldn't hear. It was a "Myster-E."

But just a minute later, *BANG,* like magic, the door flew open and in walked Mr. Prothero. He's principal of Sumac School. He's always telling us how great our school is. He's shaped like Santa Claus, but he was dressed like a principal. His suit was blue and his tie had spiders on it. You could see he was trying to hide something in his hand.

"Team," he said, "I just left an important principals' meeting to wish you good luck. I want you to give it all you've got on Saturday. Mr. Economopoulos was a chess champion in high school, and I know he's a dynamite coach. So go out and win on Saturday for Sumac School! We're counting on you!"

With that, he put his hand to his mouth. He had a harmonica. First he stamped his foot, and then he began to play. It sounded like "Twinkle, Twinkle."

We knew the right words, though, and we sang along. "Sumac School Is Best in State. Sumac School Is Really Great!"

He shook his hands together over his head like he'd just won a big wrestling match, and then *BANG*, he was gone.

Mr. E nodded. "Now, team, you need to believe in yourselves as much as Mr. Prothero and I believe in you."

He leaned over, took something from behind my ear, and gave it to me. It was the magic knight. "I think you lost this," he said.

I quick stuffed it in my chess bag before Patrick could see it.

"Thanks, Mr. E," I told him, "but I'm still not sure I can beat Harry."

"Of course you can't," he said. "Not by yourself. It'll take *four* players to beat Harry. That's because Harry isn't one person."

"Wait a minute. Is he a robot?" Patrick asked. "I'm not playing any robot."

"Harry is a team," Mr. E told us. "This is a team tournament. There'll be at least ten players there from Maple School. But only the top four scores from each team are going to count.

"The four best players at Maple play chess together almost every day. They're Hal, Alice Rea, Rashad, and Yasmin. They call themselves 'HARRY.' It's from the first letters of their names. They're the ones who made up the song."

"It takes four kids to make a HARRY?" Shasha asked.

"Wait a minute." Patrick shook his head. "You mean, if I come in fifth, my score won't count?"

"You can't be fifth on our team," Mr. E told him. "Sumac only has four players. Ben, Richard, Patrick, and Shasha."

"Well, if they're HARRY, what does that make *us?*" Shasha asked. "B-R-P-S. We're the *BURPS?*"

Patrick laughed. He was making this gross burp when the door opened. It was Ben. He smiled a little, without opening his mouth. Patrick looked the other way.

"Come in," Mr. E said. "We're just talking about Saturday. How's the tooth?"

Ben held his hand over his mouth so we couldn't see. "Dr. Todd had to cancel," he said. "He broke his big toe today. The first time I can see him is Saturday morning." He took his hand away. The tiny triangle of tooth was still gone. "That means I can't go to the tournament."

"Uh-oh. Now we're R-P-S, the *URPS*," said Shasha.

"Some team," Patrick said. "Only three kids. If it takes four scores to win, we've already lost." He crossed his arms. "Okay. That's it. I'm not going." He picked up his shoebox filled with dinosaurs.

"Uh-oh," Shasha went. "Go Team S-R . . . *SIR?*"

"A fierce dinosaur player like you, Patrick, a

quitter?" Mr. E asked him. "Would you really let your team down like that?

"It's true," he went on. "We can't win first place with three players. But I've seen the *second*-place trophy. It's so big and shiny, it looks like pirate treasure."

"Well," Patrick told him, "I guess you really do need me. We can't just send one kid who looks like she's in preschool and another one who plays with piggies and skunks. HARRY would laugh us out of there."

"Hey, I'm six years old," Shasha said. "And Richard beats you more than you beat him." She folded her arms.

"That's my lucky chess set you're talking about," I told him. I folded my arms.

"Go, team," Ben said. He laughed. "No kidding, you can do it."

"Of course you can," Mr. E said. "You three are all good players—when you concentrate on the game and plan ahead. You'll do just fine, whether you win a trophy or not. No matter what, Mr. Prothero and I and the whole school will be proud of you."

For a minute, nobody said anything.

Mr. E looked serious. "Remember, you're Team Sumac! Chess!" he shouted. He threw his arms up high. No magic flew out.

We all looked at our feet. "I love it," we mumbled. "I love it. I love it." Nobody pumped fists.

five

Go,
Team,
Go

It was a quarter till nine on Saturday morning. Tournament day. The sky was gray. It looked like rain. I was sitting on a bench in front of Maple School. I could feel the magic white knight in my pocket. Shasha and Patrick weren't there yet.

Over at the bike rack, locking up a blue bike right next to mine, was somebody I knew. Her hair was red. She had on a red checked shirt and blue jeans. I blinked my eyes to be sure.

"Ophelia?" I called. "What are you doing here?" She was all dressed up for the wedding, but this sure wasn't Heeby-Jeeby Amusement Park.

"Allergy," she said as she ran up. "I love it I love it I love it!"

"I don't get it," I told her.

"I sneezed so much, my mom took me to the doctor. Guess what? I'm allergic to *roses*. They mess up my nose. I begged and I begged. I begged like Patrick. I told my mom how much the chess team needed me, and guess what? She finally let me come.

"Besides, Mary Jo didn't want me. She said what good was a runny-nose kid who might, like, barf at her wedding? My sister Bea's going to do it.

"When I get married, I'm going to carry dandelions," she said. "You sneeze on the white ones and they make puffy little parachutes."

By the time she'd finished talking, Patrick and Shasha had both come running up.

"Are you here to play?" Patrick asked Ophelia.

"Yes!"

We did high-fives all around, like a real team.

"Now there are four of us again," Shasha said, and she gave Ophelia a big hug.

"Does Mr. E know?" I asked Ophelia.

"My mom called him last night. Where is he?"

"Inside," I told them. "We'd better get in, too."

"Wait," Shasha said. She told Ophelia about HARRY. "We can't be the BURPS anymore because Ben's gone. But we've got you, Ophelia! We've got to take away a B and add an O."

"The ORPS?" Ophelia asked.

"The ROPS," I said.

"No, no, no. We're the PROS!" Patrick said. "That way my name's first. Anyway, I'm a PRO! Like a Chicago Bull."

"The PROS," I said. "I like it." Patrick's idea or not, it wasn't bad. "We can win with a name like that."

"If we play like pros, we can," Ophelia said. "But you know, Patrick, I beat you almost every time. You want to know why? It's because . . ."

Patrick closed his eyes and put his fingers in his ears.

"Don't tell him," I said. "When I beat him, I love it I love it I love it!"

He opened his eyes.

"Me, too," Shasha said. "Do we have to?"

"Yeah, we do," Ophelia told her. "Remember, together we're the PROS. It'll take all of us to beat HARRY. Mr. E said so. Unplug your ears, Patrick. Please. If I'm going to miss cotton candy at the wedding," she said, "I want to be on a winning team."

I said to myself, "Go, Ophelia!"

"Sometimes you play really good, Patrick," Ophelia told him. "Just, please, don't get so mad when you're stuck. When you're mad, you don't think about your moves. You just think about *you*."

Patrick pulled his fingers out of his ears. "You don't know anything!" he shouted.

"Me next," Shasha said. "You know you're not supposed to talk. But you go blah-blah-blah, and that's not good."

"Ha!" he said. "Did you see me send Richard down the tube on Monday? He was out of there."

"Okay," I told him, "you did. But I beat you a lot, too."

"I get bad luck," he told us. "It's not my fault."

"Come on, we're never going to get HARRY this way," Ophelia said. "Patrick, Mr. E has told us all a trillion times to concentrate. You can't concentrate when you're mad. So I've got this idea. If you start getting mad when you're playing, imagine something that'll cool you off."

"Ice cream cools me off," Patrick went, grinning, like this was a big joke. "Ice cream, I love it I love it I love it!"

"Great," Ophelia told him. "You're in a game, okay? You start to get mad, here's what you do. You think about scooping vanilla ice cream into your mouth."

"No. I like Choco-Chunk," he said.

"Okay, Choco-Chunk."

"With fudge sauce." He laughed.

"Nuts?" I asked.

"Hold the nuts." He laughed louder. "This is nutty."

"Please," Ophelia said. "Just try it. Swallow the ice cream. Cool off. Then think hard about your moves. That's the big part. Do it for the PROS."

"This is silly," he said.

"Come on," I told him, "do it for the team!"

Ophelia turned to me. "You, too," she said.

"Ha!" said Patrick.

"We can't win unless you do, too," Ophelia went on. "You're like Patrick. You've got to think and plan."

"I know, I know," I told her. Mr. E had said it, too. "Like Patrick." I wasn't going to be like Patrick anymore. No way.

"Let's go. Let's go! We're almost late," Shasha said. She was jumping up and down.

We hurried inside and followed the big yellow CHESS TOURNAMENT signs.

"Team Sumac!" Mr. E called out as he met us. He rushed us into the multipurpose room. There were lots of kids there from five different schools. So many tables were out, it looked like lunchtime. Except they all had chessboards on them.

"Who's going to win today?" Mr. E asked us.

All four of us looked at each other. "We are!" we yelled, and punched the air with our fists.

"Okay, what do we always check out?" he went on.

"The whole board!" we yelled.

"What do we do when we see a good move?" he asked.

"Look for a better one!"

"Onward!" he shouted.

PONG! PONG! said the speakers. Somebody was thumping on a microphone. "Is this thing working?" a boy on the stage asked. Turns out it was Hal, the H guy of HARRY. He looked like fourth grade. He said everybody was welcome. Then he said the Maple players were going to sing a song.

Mr. E told us he was going to check the schedule. He told us to stay where we were, that he'd be right back.

All ten kids from Maple School lined up on the stage.

"I know what they're going to do," Ophelia told us. "They're going to sing that 'Hip, hip, hooray for Harry' thing."

"They're trying to scare us," Shasha said. "That's what."

"Let's do something back," I told them.

"Like what?" Ophelia asked. "We don't have anything."

Four of the kids on stage were each calling out their names: "Hal!" "Alice Rea!" "Rashad!" "Yasmin!" "H-A-R-R-Y. And that spells HARRY!" they yelled. And then they started in on the hair, ear, chest, and nose stuff. They tried to get all the kids there to do it.

"No way we're going to do that," Patrick said. "No way. What we do is, we go up on the stage and we say, 'We're the chess PROS from Sumac.' And we shout out *our* names so they'll know what PROS stands for."

"Okay," I said, "okay, and then . . . and then . . .

what if we just do what Mr. E always does? What if we go, 'Chess! I love it I love it I love it!'"

By this time all the kids who weren't from Maple School were feeling like they had left their brains in bed, you could just tell. They were really messing up the hair, ear, chest, and nose stuff.

After the last "Hooray for HARRY," Team Sumac marched on the stage. "Our turn," Patrick said, and he grabbed the mike from the Hal guy.

"Hi!" Patrick shouted. The "Hi!" bounced all over the room. "We're the chess PROS from Sumac School. I'm P, Patrick." We all said our names.

And then we did it. We really did it. We screamed, "Chess! I love it I love it I love it!" We pumped fists. It felt so good, we looked at each other and did it again and again. By the time we got to the end, all the kids out there were yelling with us. They were pumping their fists, stamping their feet, and screaming. The walls shook, it was so loud.

Mr. E was pumping *his* fists and yelling, too.

We were heading off the stage when Shasha stopped us and said, "Listen, it's not true."

"Hurry," Mr. E called up to us. "The games are about to begin."

"You don't love chess?" Ophelia asked Shasha.

"Oh, I do," Shasha went on. "But I said you shouldn't talk, and I do. . . . I trash-talk," she told us.

"You *what?*" Patrick asked. "No, you don't. Trash talk is what basketball players do. In the pros. They say stuff to keep the other guy from thinking about how he's playing."

"Me, too," Shasha said. "My daddy says that's what I'm doing when I play big kids in my neighborhood. Before we start, I ask if it's the knight or the rook or the queen that jumps like an L."

"You know it's the knight," Ophelia said.

"But they think I *don't* know," Shasha told her. "They think I'm a baby and that they don't have to try. It's a kind of trick. Sometimes it works." She laughed. "Better watch out in case somebody tries it on you."

"Ha!" Patrick said. "Nobody tricks me."

"Group," Mr. E called, "hurry it up."

"Shasha can trip up guys like that," I told Patrick, "but don't you go trying it."

"Me?" he asked. "No way. Nobody'd ever believe I'm not a winner."

Mr. E met us as we climbed off the stage. "That's the spirit," he said. "I'm proud of you." He handed us each a sheet of paper. It told us where to sit for our games and whether we were playing the black or white pieces.

"Now, remember," he said. "Keep your mind on the game, plan ahead, and go get 'em!"

He pulled me aside. "Richard," he said, "do you have the knight?"

"In my pocket," I told him.

"I gave him to you," he said, "because I think you're the way I was when I was starting to play. I worried so much about losing. That knight is from my very first chess set. Once I got so discouraged, I just threw my whole set in the garbage."

"Except him?" I asked.

"I found him later under my bed. His horse's leg was broken, but the knight was still holding on. It was like he wouldn't let me give up. So I kept him. I've taken him to every game since. See if he'll help you out today."

"But . . . but how does he work? Is he really magic?" I asked.

Mr. E smiled. "I thought the knight wanted me to win. I thought he could help me remember how to do it. And win I did. To me that was magic."

Then the buzzer went. It was time to play. Mr. E had to go stand at the side of the room with all the other coaches.

In the first round, I got a second-grade girl from Linden School.

"You play much?" she asked me.

I shrugged. Then I thought about Shasha's trash talk. Maybe I could try it—just for fun. "I mostly play with my Old MacDonald set," I told her. "The pawns are skunks." It was true, too.

She poked the girl next to her and whispered, "His pawns at home are stinky skunks." They laughed like I was a clown.

I took Mr. E's white knight from my pocket. "Okay, knight," I thought, "we're going to play better than she does. I just bet that you know everything Mr. E has ever taught us." I held him tight in my left hand.

With my right hand, I won. The knight and I won.

My next game was against a third grader named Jason. I told him about my skunks, too.

"Whatever," he said. "I've got a Star Wars set."

He knew what he was doing. But I stopped myself from thinking about losing. The knight and I thought about what moves Jason might make. We thought about what moves I might make.

It took Jason forty-five minutes to beat me. The knight and I tried. But everybody loses sometimes. Even knights.

The kid and I were shaking hands and saying, "Good game," when I heard Ophelia yell, "Choco-Chunk ice cream!" Kids all over lifted their heads to see what was going on.

In the middle of the room, Patrick was standing up. "It's your TURN!" I heard him say.

A couple of tables over, Shasha stood up. "Fudge sauce!" she called. Patrick looked at her. He looked at Ophelia.

He slapped his forehead like he'd just remembered something. I saw him take a deep breath. Maybe the ice cream break was working. Maybe he was listening to the team.

I squeezed the knight tight. I bet he'd want the whole team to win, not just me. I wanted that, too.

I stood up. "Hold the nuts," I said. Some kids giggled.

The next kid, I played for thirty minutes. Then he went to the bathroom. While he was gone, I studied the board hard. The knight and I put together this really good plan from stuff Mr. E had told us.

When the kid got back, he took one of my rooks. Yes! I knew he would! He did it because he could. Two moves later my queen and my other rook had his king trapped.

"Checkmate," I said. He looked down, then up. He shook his head. Then he shook my hand.

We each played three games in the morning and one game in the afternoon, with pizza in between. My last game was with Yasmin from the HARRY team. I squeezed the magic knight so hard my hand hurt. "Make the best move—not the easiest," the knight was telling me. I should have listened.

What I did was, I took one of her bishops. Taking a bishop can be a big deal, but it was a trap. I fell right into it.

After the tournament, Mr. E gave all four PROS high fives. "Great job!" he said. "But what was all that about ice cream?"

"Just a magic trick," I told him. He shook his head and laughed.

Then we sat in the front row of tables and told him about our afternoon games. He'd been on the sidelines and hadn't seen how smart or dumb we'd been.

Both Patrick and I won two of our four games. Mr. E said that was very good. "You and Patrick will both get better," he told me. "You're like two peas in a pod."

"No way," Patrick told him. "I rule."

I stared Mr. E straight in the eye. "I am not a pea in the pod with Patrick," I said. "Not anymore."

Ophelia won three games. Shasha won all four. She got a big gold trophy for being Best Kindergartener. We clapped like crazy and yelled, "Go, Shasha! Go, PROS!"

The Maple School principal, Mrs. Kim, announced the rest of the winners. "Only the second- and first-place schools will receive trophies," Mrs. Kim said. "And the second- and third-place teams were quite close. Just one point apart." The room got quiet.

She dropped her papers on the floor.

Patrick looked like he was about to tackle Mrs. Kim.

"The third-place team," she said, when she got her papers back, "is from . . . Linden School. And the second-place winners, by one point . . ." Mrs. Kim waited. She waited for what felt like thirteen hours. "The second-place winner, the runner-up in today's tournament, . . . is the Sumac School team that calls itself the PROS!"

"Yes!" Patrick yelled. He was the first one to the stage. I think he flew. But Ophelia, Shasha, and I were right behind him.

Patrick took the trophy. He hugged it. He held it out. It did look like pirate's treasure. It was shiny and silver and almost as tall as Shasha. There was a king on top. The words on the base, in fancy letters, said SECOND PLACE. And it was ours.

Everybody knew who would get the first-place prize.

"The winner," Mrs. Kim said, "is our very own . . . HARRY." Their whole team had only lost two games.

We went, "Hip, hip, hooray for HARRY." Mr. E told us to say it. "It's just good chess manners, like shaking hands and going 'Good game,'" he said. Their trophy was huge and gold.

But our silver one was almost as huge. All four

of us wanted to carry it, but Mr. E swooped it away and headed for the door. We all ran around him, yelling "Please, please."

When we got outside, the clouds were dark and low, but the silver sparkled anyway. It was awesome.

"This is our first trophy of many," Mr. E said, holding it up.

"I get to take it home," Patrick told us. "My mother has the perfect place for it. The rest of you can come look."

"That would be a no, Patrick," Mr. E said. "The team trophy will go on permanent display at school."

"Bummer," Patrick said.

"But you can show it off to your families this weekend," Mr. E told us.

"Me first," Patrick said.

"You're *last* on the list," Ophelia told him. "Shasha won the most games."

Shasha shook her head. "I'll just take mine," she said. "You fight over that one. My daddy's here." She headed toward a parked car, holding the gold trophy over her shoulder like she was trying to burp it.

"I could carry the big one on my bike, easy," Ophelia said. "It's not that heavy."

"How about me?" I asked. "I've got new tires."

A horn honked. It was Patrick's mom. "Patrick!" she called. "That's some trophy. Is it yours? Better get it over here before the rain starts."

Mr. E looked up at the sky. "Plenty of time for you to share it," he said. "Bikes aren't a good idea. The trophy's light, because it's made of plastic. It's fragile. If you drop it, it's goodbye, trophy.

"So here's the plan. Patrick, you carry it home in your car. Then tomorrow morning you take it to Ophelia's house, very carefully. Ophelia can take it to Richard's. Richard, you bring it to school on Monday. But not on your bicycle! Understood?"

We all nodded yes.

It started to rain. Patrick's mother honked again. Mr. E handed the trophy to Patrick. "I'll call and explain it to your mother. Don't run," he said.

Patrick ran.

six

Crunch!

My mom drove me to school on Monday because I had two big black garbage bags to carry. One of them I put in my locker. The other one I took very, very carefully into Mrs. Zookey's room. I was almost late.

Patrick was talking to Dawn Marie when I got there. "And this kid just gave up, I was so good," he said. He didn't even look at me. He just stuck his foot out, like always.

When Patrick sticks his foot out, I always hop over it. Almost always.

Not this time. This time I tripped.

I fell.

I landed flat on the big black bag.

Crunch! You could hear the plastic smash. I felt it crumble under me.

Kids caught their breath. Then the room got quiet.

Mrs. Zookey came running over. "Oh, Richard, are you all right? I hope those weren't your bones I heard cracking."

"Patrick tripped him," Dawn Marie said.

"I saw him do it," a kid called from Table Three.

"Me, too," said Ben.

Patrick's mouth opened. Not a sound came out.

"Did you bring the trophy?" Ophelia asked me.

Slowly, I stood up. I nodded. I rolled my eyes. The broken pieces in the bag rattled.

"But I stick out my foot every day," Patrick said, "and every day Richard jumps over it."

"I carried the trophy to school in a bag to keep it safe," I told everybody. And this was true. I did.

I had planned ahead, like a good chess player. I knew that Patrick's move would be to trip me. My move was to trick him.

By now, Ophelia was looking like she'd lost another gerbil. "Patrick," she started, "you are—"

I opened the big black bag and emptied it into the trash basket. Out fell pieces of a Darth Vader mask I got three years ago and two parts of an old lightsaber. They were already pretty busted up when I left home.

Patrick looked. His eyes went wide. He sucked in his breath. "That's not my chess trophy," he said.

"*Our* chess trophy," Ophelia told him.

"Nope. The trophy's in my locker," I told the class. "You want to see it?"

Mrs. Zookey sat down on her desk. She smiled. "I'm not sure what's happening here, but I've heard a lot about this trophy," she said. "Richard, you may go get it."

I ran out and came back in with the other big black garbage bag. Slowly, I untied the yellow bow. I pulled out our trophy, all silver and shiny.

"I can't believe it. You tricked me," Patrick said. He put his head in his hands.

"Gotcha!" I told him.

"Wow!" Dawn Marie went. "Patrick said it was big, but that thing's huge. Is it real silver?"

"It's the one the chess team got Saturday," I told them.

"Everybody's talking about it," Mrs. Zookey said. "Who can tell us about the team?"

Ophelia raised her hand and Mrs. Zookey nodded. "We," Ophelia announced, "are the PROS. P for Patrick, R for Richard, O for me, and S for Shasha. She's in kindergarten, but she's a really smart player. She got her own trophy."

"Can I tell the story?" I asked.

"We can hardly wait," said Mrs. Zookey.

I sat our mega-trophy on her desk. "On Saturday," I began, "the Sumac School chess team played all the school chess teams in town. All five of them. We almost won."

"Wait a minute. You *didn't* win?" You could see that Mrs. Zookey couldn't believe it. On her desk was this huge trophy.

"We came in second," I explained. "HARRY got first place. HARRY is the Maple School team. Their trophy was gold and even bigger than ours. They won by a lot, but not next time. Next time, we'll win first."

And that's when Mr. E came into our room. Just behind him was Mr. Prothero.

Patrick looked at me and shook his head. "Don't tell," he whispered. I shrugged my shoulders.

"Good work, chess players," Mr. E said, pointing at the trophy. "Looks as though it got here safely."

Patrick covered his ears, but I didn't tell. Nobody did.

"Good work, indeed," said Mr. Prothero. "Stand up, chess players. You have made us proud."

We stood up while he pulled out his harmonica and played a few notes on it. "Now, let's hear it for this fine team," he said. He picked up the trophy and held it high. "Hip, hip, hooray!"

"Hip, hip, hooray!" the whole class echoed him.

"Sumac School *Is* First-Rate!' Mr. Prothero called out. "Sumac School Is Best in State!" Then he waved and left, holding the trophy tight.

Mr. E stayed, though. He pointed at Ben. "Let's see your smile," he said. "Is it okay again?"

"I don't look like Dracula anymore," Ben said, and he held his top lip up. "A little piece of one tooth is fake forever, but I bet you can't tell which."

"I've got one of those," Sam said. "It hurts when you bite ice cream."

"Well, it looks as if we've started Yummy and Yucky time," Mrs. Zookey told us. "Mr. Economopoulos, unless you're too busy, you're welcome to hear a few more."

"Yes," he said, "I'd like that." He stood by the door.

"What else do you have to share before we start Science?" Mrs. Zookey asked us.

Ophelia raised her hand. "My little sister threw up on the tilt-a-whirl Saturday. But she came home with a bagful of blue cotton candy just for me."

"Zilly stole a chicken nugget right off my plate last night," Dawn Marie told us. "I said, 'Bad dog!' But he isn't. Not really. This morning he licked me awake."

"Gross," I said. "I had him lick me once. That's not a Yummy, that's a Slimy."

"Mine now, please, please, me?" asked Patrick. On the table in front of him he had his box full of dinosaur chess pieces.

"No," I said. "My turn."

Mrs. Zookey nodded to me. "But this is the

last one. Then we're on to insect-eating flowers."

"Okay," I said. "At Chess Club today, I am going to beat Patrick. And I'm going to do it using his dinosaur chess set. I don't have to use my lucky set to win."

Patrick opened his box and took out a T-rex. He waved it so everyone could see. "You wish," he told me.

"I *know*," I told him. "Mr. E," I went on, "can I tell you a secret?"

Patrick shook his head like crazy, but Mr. E bent down. I started to whisper to him, but I didn't. Instead, I took the white knight from my fist and pretended to find it behind his ear.

"Here." I gave it to him. "I still think this is magic, but I'm going to beat Patrick without it."

"Good idea," Mr. E said. He held the knight up for the class to see. "I have in my hand a magic knight," he told them. "Look closely at him. He's magic to the one who believes in him. He can help that player remember how to win at chess." He closed his fingers around the knight. When he opened them again, his hand was empty.

The kids in the class clapped because the knight had come and gone so fast.

"These two young men will play one fine game after school," he went on. "Anyone who wants to watch this epic match is welcome. I think it'll make you want to set up your own kings and queens and knights and join the club."

"GROAAAAARRR!" Patrick went, and he pointed his T-rex with the sharp plastic teeth straight at me. Then he looked down in his chess box. "Whoa!" he said. He reached in, took something out, and pointed *it* at me, too. "Is this thing really magic?" he asked Mr. E.

It was the little white knight.

"The horse has a broken leg," I told him.

Mr. E smiled. He lifted his hand to say good-bye, and suddenly there was a wand in it. He waved the wand in a big figure eight, and a rain of white paper pieces flew out. Everybody reached for them, even Mrs. Zookey.

I caught one and unfolded it. It said, "Chess! I love it I love it I love it!"

Chess! I Love It I Love It I Love It!
is Jamie Gilson's 20th
book for young readers.

Another Table Two story
by Jamie Gilson

Gotcha!
Illustrated by Amy Wummer

"This latest adventure in Gilson's schoolroom series combines a canny ear for classroom interactions—particularly those that happen without the teacher noticing—with a light-hearted tone that moderates more serious issues. . . . The deft management of dialogue . . . makes this accessible early chapter book remarkable."   —*Bulletin of the Center for Children's Books*

"Sprinkled with humorous moments, the text is fast paced and engaging. . . . In this easy chapter book, Gilson mixes fun and facts about spiders with realistic dealings with bullies."
—*School Library Journal*

"Kids will have no trouble recognizing the emotions and experiences captured by the story or Wummer's simple drawings."
—ALA *Booklist*

10/08